I0646537

Charlie And Isabella's Magical Adventure

Felicity McCullough

Series:
Charlie And Isabella's Magical Adventures

www.mylapshop.com

My Lap Shop Publishers
Plymouth, England
www.mylapshop.com

Copyright © 2011 My Lap Shop Publishers

All rights reserved.

No part of this publication may be reproduced, stored in a retrieval system, or transmitted in any form or by any means, electronic, mechanical, photocopying, recording, scanning, or otherwise, without the prior written permission of the Publisher. Requests to the Publisher for permission should be addressed to My Lap Shop Publishers, 91 Mayflower Street, Unit 222, Plymouth, Devon PL1 1SB UK

First Edition January 2012
Published by:
My Lap Shop Publishers
91 Mayflower Street, Unit 222
Plymouth, Devon PL1 1SB
United Kingdom
Tel: +44 (0)871 560 5297
www.mylapshop.com
www.goatlapshop.com

The delightful Illustrations are by Elena Shalkina and the publishers appreciate greatly her skill in interpreting the story.

The publisher thanks Nathaniel Alec for his creativity, inspiration, and contribution to content and David Brown for his support and help in bringing these series of books to publication.

ISBN - 978-1-78165-001-1

Dedication

To My Ever Loving Mother

Felicity McCullough

Somewhere deep in a big forest, there were two Angora goats that lived together.

These two goats were very special, because they were magical and kind. They could think and talk just like you and me.

Each had a coat of gold, which shimmered in the sunlight.

Charlie was a buck and Isabella was a doe.

They had lived in the forest for many years.

Charlie and Isabella enjoyed the peace and harmony of the forest.

Their home was surrounded by trees and lakes, where they could eat as much as they wanted to.

The two magical goats ate golden berries that grew in a hidden glen.

The forest was so vast that they had never seen a human before. The goats could vanish from sight in a flash.

No human had ever seen them either.

Daily, after eating the golden berries, they explored the rest of the forest.

Life was like this for them. Isabella and Charlie realised how boring it was, to do the same things each day.

Isabella began wishing that one day, something would happen to change their lives.

They had never ventured very far, as they always became distracted by browsing on a new tree or plant that they discovered.

Charlie preferred to stay near to their home. However, Isabella had always wanted to explore further afield. She was the braver goat.

One day, Isabella wished to find something new, so that she could have much more fun. Isabella decided that today was the day she was going to go further, than she had gone before.

Charlie agreed with her, even though he felt safer at home.

Charlie reluctantly followed her and they walked the forest for most of the day, barely stopping to eat.

Suddenly it grew dark. A large cloud had appeared in the middle of the sky and the forest went dark. Light was flickering and dancing across the forest floor.

Charlie became scared. He told Isabella that he was going to go home, as he wished he was safe at home, in their glade with the golden berries.

Isabella said that she wanted to go a little further.

Charlie didn't like the noise that was coming from the forest and felt scared.

Isabella was much more curious to find out from where the noise was coming. She followed the sound to where it was much louder.

Sitting under an old oak tree, was a small girl wearing a light blue fluffy hat and pink boots.

The girl was sobbing loudly and at first, Isabella felt like running away.

Isabella was curious, so she edged nearer and became less afraid. She asked Charlie, what is that? Charlie said that he did not know.

The girl on hearing voices looked up. She saw the shimmering golden coats of the two goats. She stopped crying. She was shocked that the goats could talk.

The girl said she was called Sophie.

Isabella asked what the matter was.

Sophie said that she had been out walking in the forest. It had got dark and she had become lost. She was crying because she could not find her way home.

The two magical goats felt bad for this small, crying girl.

Isabella told her they, would help her find her way back home.

Sophie began to smile and thanked the two kind goats. She became happy and played with the goats for a while. She even forgot that she was lost in the forest as she was having so much fun.

Charlie said that he would protect Sophie. He set about building a cart from some of the logs lying on the forest floor.

Very soon Charlie had built the cart. It looked magnificent.

Isabella was very impressed with the cart that Charlie had built. She was very proud of him.

The two goats harnessed themselves to the cart.

Charlie told Sophie to get in the back.

Charlie and Isabella sped through the forest and suddenly they started flying.

The two goats were surprised, as they didn't know that they had the magic powers to fly. They were very happy.

This meant that they could help Sophie to get home even quicker.

Flying high over the forest, Sophie soon spotted her house in the distance.

Charlie and Isabella safely landed the flying cart a few yards from Sophie's front door.

Sophie jumped out of the back of the cart.

Sophie began crying again.

The goats became concerned and asked why she was sad.

Sophie said she was just very happy that she had met Charlie and Isabella and didn't want to leave them.

The goats said that they couldn't stay, because they would miss their home too much.

Sophie thanked Charlie and Isabella. She waved goodbye, with tears still in her eyes.

The two sad goats did just the same.

Isabella told Charlie how brave he had been. Both smiled at each other.

They fled into the forest laughing and joking, as they went back to their golden berry glen.

They said that they would never forget the joy and memories of the adventure that they had with Sophie.

Books In The Series:

Charlie And Isabella's Magical Adventures

Charlie And Isabella's Magical Adventure

Charlie And Isabella Meet Jacob

Charlie And Isabella's Second Adventure With Jacob

These books may be obtained from the publisher:

My Lap Shop Publishers
91 Mayflower Street, Unit 222
Plymouth
Devon UK
PL1 1SB

www.mylapshop.com
www.goatlapshop.com
Tel: 44 + (0)871 560 5297

www.mylapshop.com

My Lap Shop Publishers
Plymouth, England
w w w . m y l a p s h o p . c o m

www.ingramcontent.com/pod-product-compliance
Lightning Source LLC
Chambersburg PA
CBHW041636050726
47507CB00026B/184